BURNT TOAST

JOURNEY OF A SEARED CONSCIENCE

JIM BOLTON

Burnt Toast
Copyright © 2022 by Jim Bolton

Tellwell Talent
www.tellwell.ca

ISBN
978-0-2288-7810-0 (Hardcover)
978-0-2288-7809-4 (Paperback)
978-0-2288-7811-7 (eBook)

This work of fiction is dedicated to my sons,
Chad and Cody, and in remembrance of my youngest son, Kit,
who all shared childhood memories from my employment
with the Department of Natural Resources of New Brunswick.

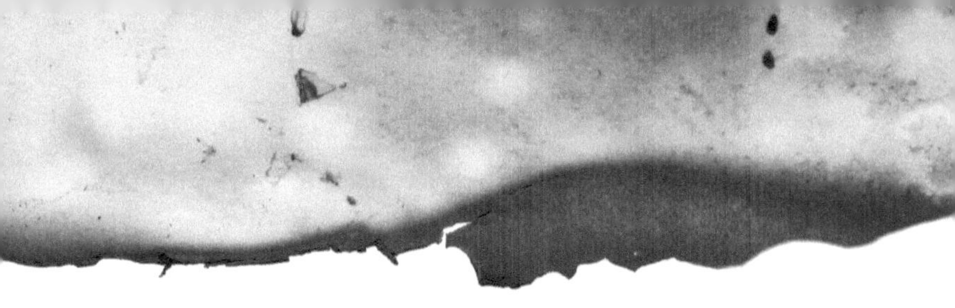

CHAPTER 1

Hasn't everyone been late? Not Ernie Doyle, ever. He detested it. He shifted to a lower gear for the approaching rise, sweat trickling down his rugged, tanned face and finding its way into his brown eyes. With a quick stroke of his right index finger, he reduced the stinging to a manageable level, his left hand piloting the ten-speed mountain bike onward. His legs churned relentlessly and his breathing remained level and unhurried, proof of his conditioning gained from years of cycling.

His annoyance at being late pushed him harder. The kids, always the kids! Life had been kind to him. At forty, he had a loving and petite wife, Kim; three sons of whom he was extremely proud (he often referred to them as the "My Three Sons" from the sixties sitcom); and a black Labrador retriever called Champ, who had to be the most brainless fleabag of a dog he had ever had the privilege of owning. The dog was a fighter, a real trooper—just ask the folks next door and their thousand-dollar purebred

German Shepherd. Or better yet, ask the vet who had to repeatedly patch him back together.

But alas, even champions have their shortcomings. His black knight had the unspeakable habit of lying down in the middle of their rural road, much to the chagrin of the local mail lady, school bus driver, and other motorists who were continually dodging the black lump as it lay sprawled out like a sunbather on a sandy southern beach. It wouldn't move, and Ernie thought that maybe this was the animal's numb concept of playing chicken with the motorized steel cages that intruded into his territory.

But on this bright morning, it wasn't the dog. The kids, always the kids. God bless their souls, but there were times when he was tempted to throw them back like unwanted chub on the end of a fishing line. He was running late, and they were to blame. Switching to a higher gear as the rise gave way to a flat stretch of asphalt, Ernie recalled the earlier events at home. He had gotten up at sunrise and attended to his usual routine of washing the night-before dishes and feeding the black wonder.

Breakfast was small—buttered toast lightly done—as this was a *travel day*, as he liked to call it. It took him thirty minutes to bike from his renovated century-old house to the district field office in Shantyville and his job as a forest ranger with the New Brunswick Department of Natural Resources. Thirty minutes to the T, which would leave him time for a quick shower and away we go, ready to face whatever the day would bring. And there had been some whoppers over his twenty years with the DNR.

He was reaching for the knob to exit his back door when he heard the thud of bare feet landing on the floor.

Five-year-old Kyle, his youngest pride and joy, came tearing around a corner headed for the bathroom. His hands were cupped gently over his groin area, and the phrase "I'm not going to make it" was bubbling from his lips.

Ernie's first two offspring, Chris and Carl, had never experienced this particular problem. The sound of soft crying caused him to pause. He took his hand off the doorknob, postponed his exit, and headed to the bathroom. Still wishful that Kyle had made it in time, he had stepped through the doorway to find the youngster holding himself, a yellow puddle at his feet and a darkening area on his pyjamas visible beneath his small hands.

Kim was sleeping soundly, as usual, when Ernie landed the recently washed and changed youngster into their rumpled bed. In retrospect, he could have awakened her so she could take care of the clean-up, but with twenty years of marriage experience he had learned it was better to come home to a happy wife. Vintage Pleasantville.

There is nothing more sinister than a woman who has been simmering all day, waiting for that perfect moment when the exhausted hubby returns home from work. But he had made his choice and was rewarded by being ten minutes late getting away to work.

"Kids," he muttered to himself. The front wheel dropped into a small pothole and the pursuant jolt brought him around to real time. As the back wheel followed the same route, he braced himself, raising his butt slightly off the seat. The jolt was slightly less aggressive than the first. Visions of Department of Transportation highway workers milling about drinking coffee, afraid to get their hands dirty, flashed through his mind. It faded fast, as he knew the public weighed his own position with the same boggling mindset: another lazy, overpaid government worker. Big bucks, no sweat! It made you want to cuff and pepper spray them until the snot choked back their jealous prejudices. The thought brought a slight smile to his face.

A hornet collided with his helmet and fell beneath his pumping legs. He was going to be late, it was that simple. It wasn't the sexual guff the guys at work would attribute to his tardiness that bothered him. Ernie just liked punctuality and routine, his life blood as a forest ranger. The conditions of work were unpredictable, and his seasoned reaction to them was organized and timely.

Pedalling into the driveway of the office, Ernie realized that he, although late, was the first staff member to arrive. The red and gold New Brunswick flag with its single-masted galley floating below a royal lion had not yet been hoisted up the pole. It was custom for the first arrival to raise the standard.

He had mused over the new provincial logo displayed on the pamphlets of angling and hunting summaries, as well as the letterhead the department used these days. The galley ship, with a new, modern look, stood alone, without the golden lion perched above her. The lion represented ties to Britain, and he envisioned the rising Acadian faction having some influence in its slaying and demise from the logo. Especially in this western rural area of the province, folks didn't take too kindly to a change of tradition, and some still flew the old Union Jack standard. There was lots of historic evidence of natural cultural change evident in the number of old and vacant buildings that used to house branches of the Orange Order, to which only Protestants could join in days gone by. Even Protestants who married a Catholic were denied membership. Every now and then there would be talk within a particular group of restarting one of the lodges. Thankfully, this never came to fruition—there was enough division in the country without piling onto it.

Propping the bike against the south-wall entrance, Ernie removed his helmet and hung it from the handlebars. He wiped his forehead with his shirtsleeve and punched in the five-digit code that unlocked the green steel door to the triple-bay compound. Inside, his sweaty fingers again entered a code to deactivate the building's security system. It took him a couple of tries as his eyes adjusted from the brightness of outside to the murkiness of the compound.

Another steel entry door with similar security hardware swung open as he entered the main office section of the building. The ranger office in times past was referred to as the "cache," but current staff had christened it "Code City." The upper floor contained five offices and a bathroom. The lower basement floor held a conference room, lunchroom, mapping room, and another bathroom, complete with lockers and shower.

The shower felt good. As he grabbed his uniform—green pants and shirt—out of his locker, he heard footsteps in the hallway above. *Great*, he thought, *some other staff have arrived. Maybe they will run the flag up the pole.* He had once loved to exercise this function, but, like anything in life, it had lost its lustre after countless repetitions. Even sex loses flavour if indulged in daily, and anybody who tells you otherwise is lying—or at least Ernie had convinced himself of this.

"Good morning, Don," ventured Ernie as he sprang up the stairs. Don Whitman was like the Maritime weather: unpredictable. His mood swings would put the Rev. Billy Graham in a feisty disposition. "See you beat me to the pole."

"Don't know why I bothered," replied Don. "Look at the limp thing. Ain't a breeze around for miles."

Don was the district forest ranger, the number one in a short line of command. Or, as Don liked to remind lesser rangers, "Look at the stripes, boys, look at all the stripes," tracing imaginary lines across his shoulder.

"It's going to be a corker, that's for sure," stated Ernie. "Temp's supposed to reach low thirties and the relative humidity around twenty-five. If we get any wind, we'll be knee-deep in trouble. With all this good weather, the campgrounds are full."

Summer tourists: city folks who are wannabe country folk. They embark on their adventure in expensive homes on wheels with about as much outdoor experience as their pampered housecats. Every summer they leave the big cities and flock to the country in an exodus of biblical proportions, revelling in getting back to Mother Nature. Most of the locals were born to the outdoors. A good laugh could always be had down at the local service station where greenhorns would stop to ask if moose, bear, coyotes, and the like lived in these woods. "Naw." Sarcastic answers were usually given. "Never saw one in the wild. There *is* a bear living at 32 Howland Ridge Road, unless all the talk about increasing the quota for the bear hunt has spooked him into moving." Stupid city-breathers. Of course, wild animals live in the wild.

"Yeah, we badly need some rain," said Don, following Ernie up the stairs and disappearing into his office. Ernie proceeded to the main office area to check on the daily class-day rating. Picking up a white sheet from the old fax machine, Ernie thought aloud, "It's got to be a three or four," and sure enough, a big bold "4" leaped out at him. He hated it when he was that right.

Four meant all available staff at the office were on fire stand-by. It was going to be a long, hot day. "Might as well tell Kim I won't be home for supper," he grumbled, reaching for the phone. Besides, it was time she was up. He was still harbouring a grudge from the morning incident. As he dialed, he pushed the number-four button on the air-conditioner with his free hand, with no results. Swearing, he slammed the phone down. Ernie Doyle detested worn-out equipment almost as much as much as he hated being late.

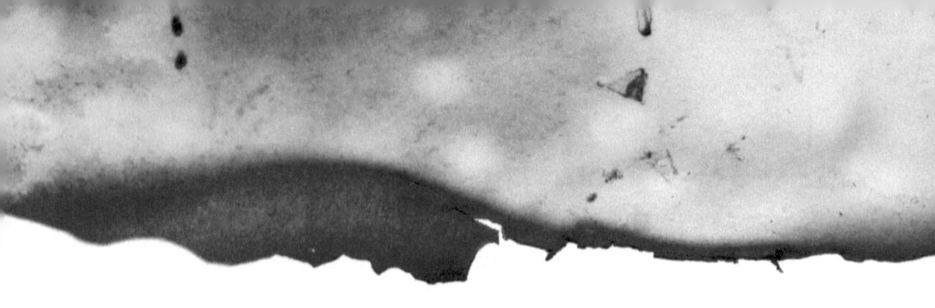

CHAPTER 2

In the gathering spots of rural Maritime villages, the watering holes and hangouts, you are likely to hear old wives' tales or delicious rumours circulating, growing with each telling and taking on new identities as each local adds their comfortable version of the truth. For the pleasant villagers of Shantyville, that place was the farmers' market, held every second Friday for the last half century. Everyone attended, but none enjoyed it more than Reginald McPhee, a hermit who lived out on Blair Ridge. Due to his prominent buck teeth and scavenging prowess, everyone from an early age had dropped "Reginald" and tagged him "Beaver."

He served in the Second World War and came home to Shantyville a shattered man. He had been found adrift in a rubber dinghy after his frigate, upon which he fulfilled the role of radio operator, was torpedoed by a German U-boat somewhere off the coast of Newfoundland. He had been afloat for days, the lone survivor. Although he had returned bodily, most of the real Beaver had not. His mental capacity was equivalent to the scrambled eggs being offered up at the market. Ironically, he was better liked by the community now than the pre-war version had ever been.

Today he was making his rounds about the market, checking out the garbage cans and grounds for discarded cans and bottles. He shuffled along on short legs, dragging a burlap bag, pausing occasional to spit tobacco juice and talk to the locals. "Not going to rain, no siree." Beaver was the self-proclaimed weatherman for the county, and his conversation was limited to this and his other favourite subject: satellite TV.

Beaver could often be found standing outside the cracked window at Reno's Hardware, hands cupped and peering through the dirty glass at the television that Reno, a gentle-spirited proprietor in everyone's opinion, left on twenty-four/seven. The rundown two-storey building, like most outlying area merchants, served a dual purpose for the village. The business was also the satellite TV agent of the region. Reno always contended he left the TV on as a means of advertising the clear reception of satellite TV, but the locals knew he did it for Beaver. Reno had come from a family of twelve and knew the world of hard knocks well. Although not related, he was kin to Beaver in this regard and had sympathy for him.

The pickings were good. Beaver smirked to himself as he perched on tiptoes to reach a partially filled soft drink bottle lying at the bottom of a trash bin. He drained the contents, licking his lips. Big-headed city folk could turn out something like satellite TV but didn't know that returnables were worth five cents. He idled by a couple of tables of preserves and followed his nose to a vendor selling hotdogs and sausages. He settled for an Italian sausage, loading it with ketchup and mustard. Scarfing down his treat, and with his sack nearly filled, he booted out of town and turned left onto Highway #124 towards Blair Ridge, and the shanty he called home.

Tomorrow he would lug his loot back to town and cash in. Saturday was the day Connie worked at Durling's Service Station and she would tally for him. It wasn't that Beaver didn't know the numbers, he just liked to see Connie leaning over, her ample bosom revealed as she reached into the bag, counting out loud, "One, two, three, four, five . . ." It was almost as good as satellite TV.

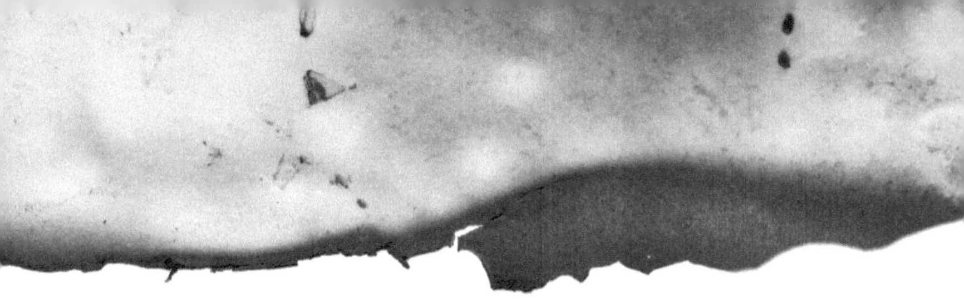

CHAPTER 3

One hundred and fifty miles to the south of Shantyville, in the fastest-growing hub in the province, sprawled the city of Sutton, which, in the opinion of its inhabitants, was the real capital of New Brunswick, thumbing their noses at Fredericton. Frederick Martin, tagged "Flammable Fred" in hushed conversations between his co-workers, gazed in disbelief at the pink slip in his trembling hand. His employment at Nor-East Cardboard Ltd. had come to an end, and frustration was swirling in his already overloaded noggin.

Management had finally learned of his secret pastime of setting fires in the company washrooms. He would enter a stall and unwind the toilet paper until it reached the tiled floor. He would hesitate after striking the match, holding it like a painter completing the final stroke of a masterpiece. No longer able to contain himself, and with the match almost spent, he would ignite the perforated single-ply edge, shouting, "Burn, baby, burn!" and watch the growing flame in awe.

Rumours were he had worked at some chicken farm up north until a major fire, which the local paper headlined as a BARBEQUE BONANZA, levelled the operation. He was questioned, but there was no hard evidence and he walked away.

Flammable Fred was a massive man with a brutish personality. He frequented bars and pool halls, where fistfights swelled his ego. His coworkers avoided him, thinking if they left him alone he might go away. Finally, a brave soul had informed the upper echelons of Fred's bathroom exploits and a coloured slip had been issued, now held fast in his shaking hand. Formally it listed "market slow-down" as the reason for dismissal. With the slip was his last cheque and final chance to pay the overdue rent on his derelict apartment. He drank most of his earnings and had fallen in arrears. Retribution whelmed up inside him, seeping out his pores and awakening mocking voices from deep within. He stomped out of the lunchroom, still with slip in hand, and the door swung shut on his departure. Everyone breathed in relief.

Two days later, a massive fire engulfed the Nor-East Cardboard plant. It was a fireball that the municipal fire department chief suspected started somewhere in the rear of the building, near the lunch and washroom area. Thankfully, it happened in the early evening while employees were at home watching the news. It was quite a blaze, drawing spectators by the hundreds, and police had a struggle to keep the crowd back a safe distance. The veteran sergeant in charge loathed disaster thrill-seekers.

Comments like, "When do the fireworks begin?" really infuriated him. He even heard some wacko from the crowd utter the phrase, "Burn, baby, burn!" Geez, he needed a vacation. Today, he wished he had listened to his father and become a certified general accountant in his firm, but no, he, like most teenagers, ignored his father's plea.

Flammable Fred tramped down Prince Street on this July evening for a couple of blocks, pausing in front of a new construction site. Tall steel girders edging skyward indicated work had just begun. An eight-foot-high wall constructed of second-grade plywood ran along the sidewalk, separating pedestrians from the work. It had received some attention from graffiti artists and commercial advertisers, along with several yard-sale signs.

His first attempt to climb the obstacle didn't succeed, his heavy bulk a burden. On his second jump, his fingers caught at the first joint and he hung for a couple of seconds, muscles bulging, unable to pull himself over the top. As he released his grip, his body rubbed on the wall, releasing several advertisements. He landed awkwardly and fell backwards like a chopped tree. Sitting on the concrete walkway amid his recent litter and swearing profusely, his eyes came to rest upon a colourful ad.

The picture displayed a young family roasting marshmallows around a brilliant yellow campfire that flared and danced upward, struggling to escape its rocky prison. It captivated him, like a stray deer caught in the headlights of an approaching car. He drew a deep breath and read on:

TIRED OF CITY LIFE? NEED TO GET AWAY?
COME STAY WITH US!
EXPERIENCE THE OUTDOORS. HIKE, FISH, BIKE, OR SWIM,
THEN RELAX AROUND THE CAMPFIRE.
YOU'LL FIND IT ALL HERE AT SHANTYVILLE
CAMPGROUNDS & LODGE.

There were further directions and a description of the facilities and prices offered. At the bottom of the ad, in bold letters, it read, FARMER'S MARKET EVERY SECOND FRIDAY.

The wooden wall dissolved into a distant memory and Fred marched away with purpose, disappearing down a meaningless street of the pretend capital of New Brunswick.

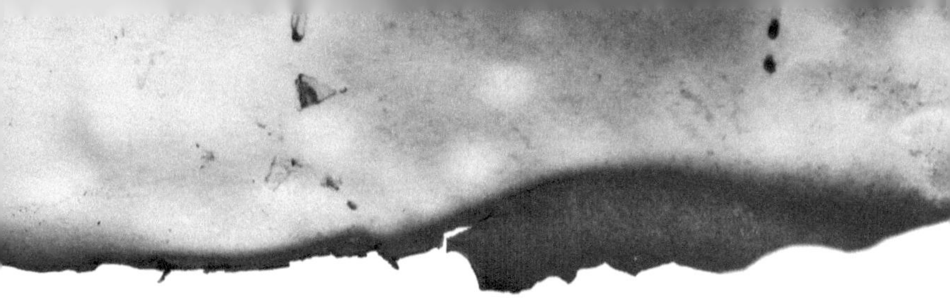

CHAPTER 4

Ernie Doyle glanced at the time on the wall: two forty-five p.m. He returned his gaze to rest on the unobstructed view of Highway 123 as it wound its way west to the Maine border.

Eighty-five percent of forest fires begin between three and six p.m., and Ernie understood why. It wasn't the fact that it was the hottest and driest part of the day, but rather that the recreational retreads were most active during this period. Forestry was important in these parts, so the wood contractors and their workers recognized the dangers of dry timber and took precautions. There were two reasons for this, the first being the safety of their crews, and the second being this was their livelihood, their bread and butter. Fires were started by numbskulls.

Movement caught his eye, and he turned his attention to a solitary figure coming up the highway. He recognized old Rudy immediately. He was of slight build, and his familiar baseball cap adorned his lowered head. Ernie puzzled over how the cap stayed on. Nobody knew Rudy's last name, not even the folks down at the special care home where he laid his head come nighttime. He was pegged Rudy Walker by ranger staff who would see him go by on multiple daily walking excursions. Everyone around town thought him simple. Ernie suspected him to be dangerously simple.

On a few occasions he had found Rudy in the vicinity of some nasty grass fires, all of which had begun close to the roadside. The reports had been filed as someone discarding a cigarette or match out of a passing vehicle, but nevertheless Ernie had asked Rudy some questions concerning them. He'd had more productive conversations with his five-year-old, and arrived at nothing tangible after questioning Rudy.

He recalled a couple of years back when, on patrol in his forest service half-ton, he had come upon Rudy and Beaver in a rock-throwing slugfest. It wasn't a friendly competition, as both were standing on either side of the road and letting them rip. Beaver had the better aim but Rudy was chucking harder. Neither had scored a serious hit, and when Ernie blared the siren of his truck both nearly came out of their skins, with Rudy losing his balance and toppling into the ditch. He chuckled to himself that Shantyville had the Nutcracker performed all year long.

"Should have stayed out of it," muttered Ernie, glancing again at the slow-moving hands of the clock. "A good stoning might have knocked some sense into old Rudy's head." The air conditioner in the office hammered away. Amazing how the thing worked better when plugged in. His first assessment of worn-out equipment had left him a bit embarrassed in the face of such a simple solution.

Ernie shuffled paperwork around on his desk, his thoughts disturbed by the tension he was feeling in his home life. He could not put his finger on why, but lately he found himself in no hurry to get home from work. He glanced out his window again and perceived that Rudy had moved out of sight. His eyes returned to the paperwork but not his thoughts. Perhaps he was overtired, or perhaps tired of his complacency at home. Usually a man who liked routine, he ventured that his lack of stimulation with Kim was a common occurrence at some point in a marriage. She had always been passionate about her community involvement, but recently most of her personal time and energy was absorbed in some sort of group event, and he felt neglected, maybe even lonely.

Don Whitman came into the front office, sweat pooling on his forehead and slowly trickling down his disgruntled, weathered face. The air conditioner was just a small unit, not capable of providing relief for the other offices down the hallway. He handed Ernie a sheet of paper soiled with perspiration. "Everything's sticky," he muttered, disappearing back into his oven-baked office. A small sheet of paper had attached itself to the seat of Don's green cargo pants like a leach, causing Ernie to grin as he recalled an early summer problem with a rodent in the attic of his home. At first, he had assumed the pest to be a mouse and had bought several of those traps that supposedly catch the invader with its sticky yellow surface. The critter, he later discovered, was a red squirrel. He spotted it jumping from the maple tree onto the roof and scurrying under a piece of loose soffit. He had forgotten all about the traps, as the squirrel had eventually left the attic, probably due to the extreme heat the summer months had brought. Then, one fateful day a few weeks back, Kim had requested—demanded, actually—that he go into the attic—the motherlode of yard-sale trash, in Ernie's humble opinion—and look through some boxes for hand-me-down clothes for Kyle. The heat in the attic was intense. Holding a flashlight in one hand while shuffling boxes around, he had stepped on one of those long-forgotten traps.

He lifted his foot, bringing with it the trap. Reaching back, he attempted to pull it from his sock. Kim always insisted that footwear was made to be worn outside, not inside, so Ernie had approached the errand shoeless. The trap wouldn't budge. Digging his fingers around the edges, he pried it off, leaving great strands of a yellow taffy-like substance connecting his fingers to his sock. What a mess.

Try as he might, he couldn't dislodge the substance from his fingers or his foot. His mind traced back to a grade three reader and the story of Br'er Fox trapping Br'er Rabbit with a child sculped from tar. These traps should be passed on to the military, as they would be more humane and just as effective as land mines and a whole lot less costly. Not that the savings would be passed on to the taxpayer, he thought, heavens no: most government department managers figured on spending their entire budgets, whether on necessary purchases or not. The military would probably just buy more of those army meal-ration packages. Ernie considered that might not be such a bad deal; he had purchased some at an army discount store and found them useful when working in the field. On top of that they were tasty, his favourite being the Salisbury steak.

The outcome was never in doubt—squirrel: one, forgetful human: zero. It took paint thinner to remove the guck from his hands. Both socks ended up in the trash because, like his grandmother used to say, what are you going to do with one good sock? Ernie figured that if life was even a bit fair, that shady garbage man he always suspected of rummaging through his trash might open that morning's garbage bag. Ernie wished he would, and may God have mercy on him. The image caused him to laugh.

On the paper Don had given him was a complaint in scrawled letters from Moose Grant about why the campground would allow campfires in light of the current fire index being so dangerous. The current level stood at five on a scale of one to five, so conditions were extreme.

Moose, whose real name was Silky (little wonder he preferred Moose), was a man with a giant chip on his shoulder. His continual negative tirades about the civil service, politicians, neighbours, and every other human being on the earth, along with his huge resentment of life in general, filtered into every conversation on any topic. People avoided him like seniors do hard toffee. His speech was slow and drawled out, much like a forty-five record played at thirty-three speed. Put plainly, he was as agitating as a visit from a Jehovah's Witness.

However, in this case Moose had a legitimate complaint. Ernie would have to take a trek out to the facility and check into whether the campfires were open-pit or contained.

"Going out to the campground at Shingle Lake," Ernie informed Don.

"Yup," replied Don in his usual unexcited voice. "The rest of the crew is downstairs, so I suppose we can manage here."

Ernie continually wondered how a man who couldn't make a clear decision and lacked the respect of staff had ever gotten to the top rung of the ladder. He figured the man was so lazy he would trip over the centre line of the road given the chance. Go figure. It's little wonder Don is unmarried. No woman would put up with that ineptness.

Climbing into his half-ton, he found the vinyl seat extremely hot. Ernie rolled the window down on the driver's side in an attempt to cool it down. The department's approach concerning vehicle purchases was a festering wound with DNR staff: all vehicles were not to have air conditioning. In fact, they were removed from vehicles prior to delivery. This logic originated with some red-tape bureaucrat from the city who thought that staff might spend too much time in their trucks instead of being out in the field on hot days. From that came the old cliché: "What is big and green and sleeps three? A Department of Natural Resources or Transportation truck." Ernie figured it originated with some stuffy wire-rim-glassed, three-piece-suited manager who would not know a spruce from a fir. City folk do not appreciate how hard country folk work to provide what they take for granted. Ask city folk where furniture comes from and they will answer the furniture store downtown.

In any case, air conditioning would have been beneficial and productive in accomplishing the many duties of a forest ranger, but the red tape did not care.

He followed Highway #123, enjoying the sunshine despite the heat. This section of road snaked its way west toward Bordertown, an isolated spot bumping up against the state of Maine, where all fifty-six of its inhabitants burned American gas and drank Yankee milk. They rarely saw each other during the long, cold winters. Most of them were snowbirds.

Halfway between Shantyville and Bordertown lay Shingle Lake, nesting site of the Shantyville Campground. The lake was freshwater and part of the Chinook chain of waters that held excellent bass and land-locked salmon populations. As Ernie pulled into the gravel driveway leading to the pine-log-constructed campground office, he tucked his shirt neatly into his pants and stroked his brown hair back, checking his appearance in the rear-view mirror.

Jessica Forbes, the sole owner of the campground and lodge, was a lovely, amusing, unattached woman of thirty years. She was the Queen of Sheba out in these parts, the kind of woman you took notice of and always wanted to look your best around. She could melt ice in the middle of winter and was every local male's dream girl. Jessica was a cool drink of water on a hot, dry day.

Lightly stepping from his truck, Ernie gave the area the onceover with his discerning eye. He hated how dead and brown the grass was. It made a crunching sound with every step, hard evidence that the sun was drying things out severely. He sent a silent prayer to any deity listening to please send some rain.

Ascending a couple of steps and opening the door to the office, he heard her pleasant laugh. She was chitchatting with a middle-aged couple and glanced approvingly at Ernie as he entered. Those blue eyes pierced him, exposing his soul, causing him to blush as if she had just read his most secret thoughts. "Hi there, handsome," she said, bringing him out of his trance. She was all woman, and she knew it.

His professionalism surfaced and he sauntered over to the long counter. "How's things in the tourism business?" he ventured.

"Almost a full house," she mused. "Business is great." She seemed pleased to see him. Maybe he was mistaken, but lately he had sensed a little more flirtation than usual. It pleased him immensely, which bothered him even more. He thought of Kim, but the image was like a frontal attack on a crowning forest fire with a squirt gun.

"Well, that's great," he ventured deeper, probing for a more personal conversation. "How about yourself? Everything good?"

"Things are better now," she replied, smiling brightly. "It's comforting to know you're around." She paused, seeing his reaction. "You know, with the hot weather and fire danger so high."

Of course that's what she meant. With a forced authoritative voice, he explained, "I got a complaint about campers burning in the fire pits." He was going to add, Thus the reason for the visit, but didn't, although that was a partial truth. The full truth lay barely covered: he relished their interactions.

"Am I under arrest?" Jessica laughed, then in a serious tone explained that all the campfires in the campground had been banned. She promised to check if this prohibition was being dutifully enforced by her staff.

Ernie stressed the dangerous level of the forest fire index. "With the index this high, I would really appreciate that. The last thing either of us needs is for me having to charge you for a violation of the Forest Fire Act." She studied him, those blue eyes holding him in place. An unspoken understanding existed that he would not really charge her. He avoided eye contact with her. Something was happening, and it alarmed and excited him, all in the same breath. It was like an undeclared union had been forged between them. Not certain what to say, and his work mission accomplished, he headed for the door. She reined him in with her soft voice.

"Don't be so long between visits, Ernie. I really am afraid of the damage a major fire in this area would do, and I feel better knowing you're about, doing your job. Drop in anytime. I love a man in a uniform, especially one who isn't afraid of a little heat." She gave a queenly wave and smiled sweetly.

He fumbled with the doorknob, and as he stepped outside the blast of heat wasn't nearly as hot as the inferno he'd experienced inside. New sweat broke out as he hopped back in the cab. The truck was just as hot, but this time Ernie didn't notice as he headed back east on the #123, lost in arousal. Somewhere along a section of the highway, he passed a brute of a man walking with purpose in the direction he had just left.

CHAPTER 5

The local village council had dubbed Shantyville the "Gateway to Heaven," due to its natural scenery and many picturesque waterways. Locals figured it coincided with the fact that there were, count 'em, not less than seven churches serving a buffet of congregations. From the three denominations of Baptist to the sister Catholic churches on the hill and the Presbyterians in the valley, there was no reason to miss Church come Sunday. If that didn't shake your wagon, then the Pentecostals' brand of holy laughter and dream interpretation was offered up Jiggertown way.

Some churches had services twice a day, and others preached only once but practically all day long. With all that holiness you would think Shantyville would be a quiet, loving, trusting place, and on its surface it appeared like that. But there was bitterness and deep-seated hate that people kept bottled up that would periodically bubble over the brim.

Country folks, though usually kind-hearted and pleasant, often festered over ill deeds performed decades ago. Undoubtedly it was a hillbilly mentality nurtured through the ages, and Shantyville's version of a feud was the Grants and the Wrights.

Families are like chip-sealed roads: they naturally stick together. If you affront one member, you affront them all. If Grandpa had been slighted, for example, the grudge was laid against all members of that offending family, like it or not.

Sam Wright was the best hater of all, and he took family feuds to a whole new realm. His primary aim within the despised Grant clan was levelled on Moose. Despite being short, Sam's odium burned long, his loathing seeping out from between his black, cracked, and worn teeth.

The wrong itself, an unreturned axe, was committed so long ago that it could be considered antique. The grudge work had been laid and developed over time to become a required element of the family heritage. It continued to this day and included a long list of untried crimes. Sam had nurtured the hatred with covert slyness, so when things appeared to be cooling off between the families another incident would arise, bringing the hate back to its natural position in the circle of life.

In a sick irony, he had on many occasions fashioned happenings against his own clan to rekindle the rivalry between the families, but what would you expect from a man, who every blessed morning would bend his ear to hear the snap, crackle, pop of his favourite cereal, morning after morning, year after year, in endless repetition?

Just a few days after Ernie's visit with Jessica, Sam crouched low to the ground, rubbing his soiled hands together with gleeful joy. It was like Christmas in July, and Sam's latest grudge work was about to be played out. He arrived at Moose Grant's house a few ticks before ten o'clock in the evening. His arrival was announced by the baying of Moose's Husky, Gabby, chained in the dooryard. He had pulled his ancient Chevy over about a mile back, hiding the vehicle on an old portage road. His trek through the timbers had been noisy, the branches cracking and snapping to denote his journey. Usually a stealthy hunter, Sam cursed silently at the noise he was manufacturing. He had never seen the woodland so dry in all his sixty-three years.

He waited patiently for the animal to settle down. Good ol' Moose, he had come to the window just once for a glimpse of what the dog was barking at. "Stupid fool," muttered Sam. It takes the eyes a couple of minutes to adjust to the darkness of the night, but Moose probably figured the mutt had heard a deer and didn't allow himself enough time to investigate what had come a-calling.

Reaching into the deep pockets of his coveralls, Sam uncovered his latest works. Wrapped in shiny tinfoil was a meatball about the size of a golf ball. In total he was carrying six of them, and each contained his special recipe. Sam had laboured over his latest dish the previous day, and as tasty as the morsel was, the malicious technique encompassed wrapping grapes with hamburger and freezing them so they would maintain their shape. He drew a little closer and threw the meatballs at the dog.

The ignorant hound gulped down the tasty treat between growls cast at Sam's hidden position.

Sam felt little sorrow for the animal, though he knew that, as the stomach and intestines warmed and digested the meal, the grapes would excrete a toxin that was deadly for dogs. Death would be painful, but the animal wouldn't last too long. The anguish that Moose would feel over his pet's demise stroked Sam's warped purpose. He stuffed the anonymous note claiming credit for this horrendous act into Moose's mailbox, and even took the time to hoist the little red tin flag. There were only four lines:

Mister, can your dog come out to play?
Or has he gone on his way
Revenge is sweet, so I slay
Expect the worst again some day!

The grudge work was laid. An interesting thing about grudges—you don't have to be a very big person to carry them.

Retracing his steps through the forest, Sam approached his hidden car. Gleefully satisfied with his recent deed, he reached for the driver's door. He detected movement out of the corner of his eye and heard shuffling feet breaking twigs on the forest floor. He turned far too slowly toward the source, and strong, rough hands closed about his neck. Sam was a fighter, but he could not break the iron grip as his body was lifted skyward.

Images flashed through his air-starved mind. The last snapshot had the despised Moose Grant standing by a casket looking down, taunting the dead. It didn't take a Mensa member to figure out who lay in the casket, and then came Sam's mother's voice taunting him, "You reap what you sow, young man, you reap what you sow." There was a loud snap and Sam passed to the other side, to come a-grudging no more.

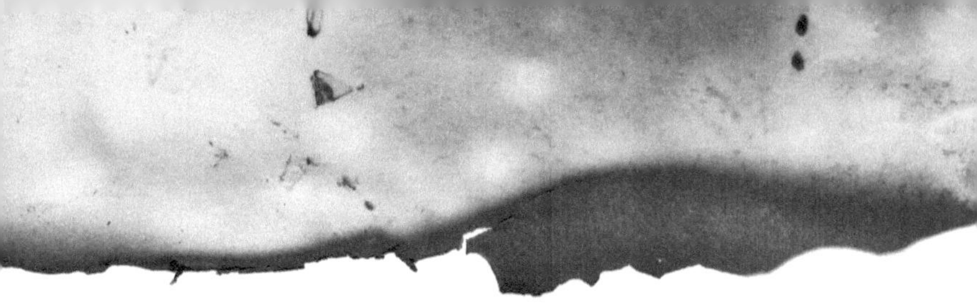

CHAPTER 6

The local detachment of the Royal Canadian Mounted Police was housed in the former bank building on Main Street in the heart of the village. With the closure of the last two sawmills, the board of directors for the bank, none of which were local talent, had relocated the company to a town with more promise.

Two new officers worked out of the RCMP sub-unit detachment, with central headquarters located in Woodside, twenty miles to the north. Lieutenants Jake Furrow and Shawn English were the latest transferees to this post, and after only six months, were still struggling with the local culture. Nothing in the academy had prepared them for the Jekyll and Hyde façade that rumbled beneath the surface of the smiling citizens of Shantyville. The previous officers' tenures had been short. Anyone assigned to this village took the first opportunity to get out of Dodge.

Before them stood an incensed Moose Grant with wildly flailing arms, demanding action for the ghastly deed committed on his dog. Moose had rushed his stricken pet to the vet in the early morning hours, only to witness its demise on the operating table. There was sorrow for the departed animal and anger over the vet's outrageous bill, but even greater fury for this attack against his personal property.

The telling note lay on an old steel desk, behind which was seated Lieutenant Furrow. His counterpart, Lieutenant English, stood to the side, plucking at his moustache and staring vacantly into space, his thoughts on the upcoming night and his date with the video lottery terminal at the neighbouring pub. His latest job transfer had aided his gambling problem, because, outside of deer-jacking, the nightlife in Shantyville was non-existent. He was trapped in this two-bit village with its unrelenting and bizarre mentality.

Jake Furrow listened to the rantings of Moose, interjecting now and then to ask a question. The result was a promise to investigate and perhaps to question Sam Wright, whom Moose had pegged as the likely villain. As Moose stomped out of the building, Jake heard him mutter something along the lines of, "Old geezer. He'll get his due, mark my words. This has gone on long enough."

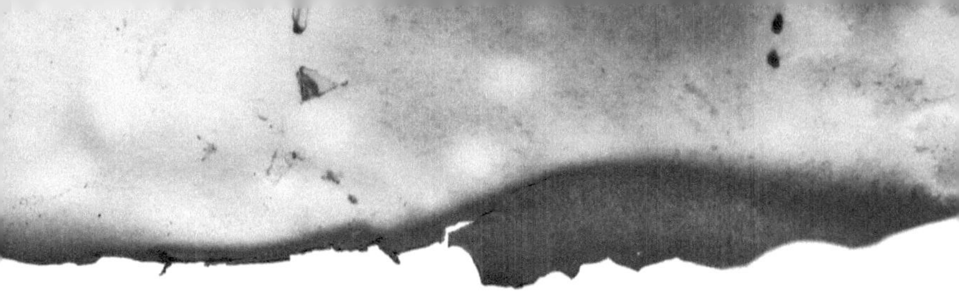

CHAPTER 7

Ernie picked up the ringing phone on the following day—yet another scorcher. It was almost noon and the fire index had reached all-time records. Not since 1965, with the big blow-up out by Sullivan Lake, had numbers like these been posted in relation to humidity and temperature.

A memo came down the pipeline from the fire centre, heavily supported by the Minister of Natural Resources, closing hunting season for all species and a ban on woodcutting operations and recreation travel. Everyone had to be out of the woods from noon to eight p.m., no exceptions. The ban was being carried out by natural resources staff, who were well aware of the high costs associated with major fires. It could run into millions of dollars that the province didn't have, so staff took this directive very seriously.

The caller informed Ernie that he had spotted an old Chevy off Crow Hill Road, parked along the old portage carriageway. The only other detail supplied was that the vehicle looked like Sam Wright's, who the caller figured was doing some illegal hunting once again.

The commander-in-chief had his feet up and was snoozing peacefully when Ernie walked by his office. Shaking his head in wonder, Ernie pondered how in the world Don had won out over him for the head position in the unit. "Connections," he mumbled to himself.

Promotions were few and far between in the department, and Ernie rationalized that the decisions on these competitions were usually based on who you knew, rather than what. Though times were changing, politics of some stripe was part and parcel of hiring. In times past, a change of political parties would lead to a wholesale turnover of staff. You could always tell what party was in power by the heavy equipment in service at the Department of Transport facility.

He was tempted to wake Don but the urge passed, because what did it matter anyway? Ernie would take a drive out to the area and see firsthand if anyone was in violation of the ban. Informing Bert, one of the two seasonal wardens, of where he was heading, he jumped into his truck and started out.

As he manoeuvred through the main part of the village, Ernie replayed the previous night's doings in his head. He and Kim had desired some much-needed snuggling, and with three kids, that kind of time was rare to find. Their alibi to the kids was that Mom and Dad were planning a special vacation for the family and needed to be alone to work out the details. The kids filled in the location, assuming the long-overdue trip was to Florida and Disneyland. They couldn't get out of their parents' way quick enough.

Ernie lay quietly at the end of the planning session, his mind and heart locked in battle over the proverbial "grass is greener on the other side" dilemma. He wanted more and didn't know how to tell her. Their lovemaking was okay, their first in months, but not really fulfilling. He wanted that breathtaking sensation that he felt—dare he think it—when *she* was near.

He almost hit old Beaver, who was crossing the street toward Reno's. Beaver, much like his name implied, was not the fastest-moving person alive, but he showed marked improvement when he saw the truck bearing down. Ernie hadn't even touched the brake when he went flying by and glanced in the side mirror to see Beaver giving him the royal salute. "Crazy old coot! What are you doing?" Ernie then addressed himself. "Slow down, concentrate, stop behaving like a teenager with his first crush. Quit daydreaming and get back to reality." In his heart he knew he still loved Kim, but the latest encounter with Jessica continued to gnaw away at his being, leaving him lost and confused. He swore softly under his breath.

From Crow Hill Road he swung right onto the portage carriageway road—if you could still call it a road, for vegetation had narrowed the sides of the right-of-way to the point where it was single-lane traffic. Not that any volume of vehicles ever used this road, mind you. Twenty metres away, an old chevy, which Ernie was now sure belonged to Sam Wright, blocked any further advance.

Climbing out, Ernie banged his door against some small poplar saplings. If he had been a bigger man, he wouldn't have been able to squeeze out between the door and the re-gen that was quickly reclaiming the roadway. He approached Sam's car, an old Nova, expecting to find zilch.

He figured that Sam, whose activities were well known by ranger staff, was probably in the vicinity scouting for the upcoming fall hunt. The staff was well aware of Sam's obsession for poaching deer and moose, and last fall they came within a whisker of apprehending him on a night-patrol stakeout. Don, as usual, had failed to see the necessity of blocking off a secondary road, thus leaving a hole in an otherwise tight web that would have good ol' Sammy's name inking the pages of this year's licence-restricted list for the province. Ernie had argued savagely to bring in outside help to aid in the setup, but Don had drug his feet, insisting he had adequate manpower in place. "Bullcrap!" Sam, like a crafty snake, had wiggled his way out through the hole, leaving the Rangers with wasted time.

Walking to the driver's door, he saw Sam seated inside and slouched against the steering wheel. His head lay at an unhealthy angle, and Ernie knew something terrible had happened. It wasn't humanly possible to do this damage to yourself, so his immediate conclusion was that somebody else had committed this ghastly act. He opened the door and pulled gently on Sam's shoulders, easing his body away from the wheel. Sam's balding head swivelled around, his open eyes fixed skyward as if in his final moments he had been hoping for heavenly intervention.

He felt for a pulse but it was an instinctive act only, for he knew Sam was gone. On shaky legs, he radioed base on his portable. With an effort, he willed himself to remain calm, to keep his voice normal. Inside, his constitution was crumpling, an unwelcome chill running up his spine despite the heat. Someone out there had done this. It had to be a man of great strength to snap a neck. It looked like it had been stretched like a strand of dough. The crack of the radio got his attention.

"Ten-four, I'm at my twenty-three now, and requesting assistance to my twenty. I've got a probable ten seventy-one," he said, his voice quivering slightly. "Give the RCMP a call and direct them to me." With the image of Don asleep in his chair oblivious to this gruesome discovery, he added with bitter contempt, "Wake the old fart and give him my location."

He cased his portable radio and took a look around Sam's vehicle. Nothing caught his attention. The car he would leave for the Mounties. His forte was fires, fish, and game, not murder. He bided his time writing notes in his green pocket diary. He didn't think Sam had been dead that long, but his experience was based on dead wildlife, so the correlation might not be that accurate.

The sirens pierced his thoughts, and he earnestly wished he hadn't come to work this day. A cold, hard fact kept breaking the surface: somewhere in Shantyville was a heap of nameless trouble.

The cavalry arrived. Ernie quickly filled Lieutenant Furrow in on his findings and retreated to his vehicle. He stifled a snicker as he backed his truck out the portage road. Don had finally arrived and was in deep conversation with Lt. English, who glanced up as Ernie drove past. Rolling his eyes, English nodded at Ernie.

Ernie figured he was getting all the advice he would never need from his boss. It's ironic that people who generally have a lot to say know the least. Ernie wasn't about to give any satisfaction to Don and simply passed by, pretending not to notice his obvious gestures to stop. There was a long line of emergency vehicles stretching along Crow Hill Road, but his wasn't going to be one of them. He glanced in his rear-view mirror to see Don still waving his arms, and gunned the truck back toward Shantyville.

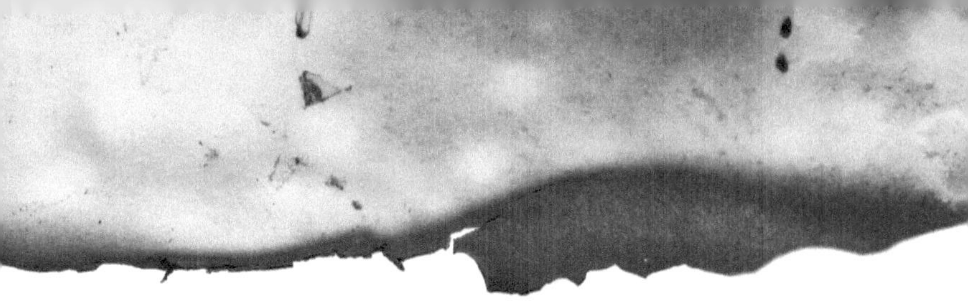

CHAPTER 8

Flammable Fred had hitched his last ride into Shantyville from Gary Durling, who owned the local service station. "A loaded cannon," he would later tell his wife. Gary had picked up many a thumber, but this guy was a couple of bricks short of a load, and he was thankful when he finally dropped the fellow off at the service station and pointed him in the direction of the campground at Shingle Lake.

The weirdo had repeatedly pointed to an advertisement for the lodge. Hardly a word had passed between them the whole trip along the Saint John River Valley, and Gary promised himself that this was his last hitchhiker. The vacant look in Fred's eyes would keep the sandman from a narcoleptic, and Gary tossed and turned most of the night before he reluctantly got up and turned on the tube.

Hiking along the #123, it took Fred the better part of two hours to reach his destination, and to his closed mind, he met and saw nothing. He might as well have been rolling along on a treadmill, for his big boots paused only at the base of a big white and green sign welcoming folks to Shantyville Campground and Lodge. Euphoria welled up inside.

Fred approached the front desk. Jessica, who had spotted him on entry, had a nose for trouble and he reeked of it. "Like a site," he demanded in a pitched voice.

"Yes, I can help with that," she ventured. "Do you expect to stay long?"

"Maybe," he replied. Then, as if he had just noticed her, he gave her a good look-over before replying, "You're a sweet thing."

Discrimination is against the law, but sometimes you wish choices could be arrived at without suitable justification. Jessica Forbes needed a reason to say no to Fred but you don't deny service to someone based on intuition. She relented with a forced "thank you," searching for a loophole to say no but coming up empty.

Paying in cash and taking a campsite down the southside of the lake, he gave another long and approving stare, turned, and exited the office. Jessica trembled as a cold shiver ran down her body, and it lingered long after he had gone.

Fred seemed content to plant his rump on the well-used picnic table near his firepit. He hardly moved a muscle, just pierced the universe with that vacant stare. A closer examination would have revealed more goosebumps striving for space on his skin.

He sat all day in the sun, unmoveable, uncaring, unattached, for he knew that when the sun dipped down, darkness would come, and he, Freddy Martin, Lord of the Flame, would bring the Mona Lisa of all campfires.

When Fred got excited as a youngster, his long-gone mother would slap him upside his head, yelling for him to quit the goose pimples. Even now he forced himself not to cringe in expectation of the slap that would never come. Unbeknownst to Fred, his mother had died by the hands of a John who testified to police that he had "slapper her around a little bit, but she was still breathing when I finished with her." Medical records showed multiple breaks on her arms and ribs, and she had died from extreme blunt-force trauma to the head.

But all that was a world away from Shingle Lake, where Flammable Fred sat on his perch, receiving strange looks from passing campers who couldn't fathom this big man with the detached smile sitting like a king on his splintery throne.

Fred finally left his sitting place in the early evening, eagerly gathering small sticks as kindling for his anticipated show. He wanted the flames to dance and reach for the sky, and he understood the need for larger wood. He headed toward the main office, where that sweet thing he had met earlier had registered him. Fred thudded into the log office, intent on seeing Jessica and buying more than a few bundles of the bigger round wood that was piled up against the exterior wall of the office. Jessica watched him enter and was instantly nervous, her intuition holding true. "How much for four bundles of round wood?" he asked, his voice strained as if he had been holding his breath before speaking.

She had dealt with many visitors to the campground, but it was not difficult to put into words what she sensed:

insanity, and that was being kind. His stare chilled her to the bone. She spoke hesitantly. "I'm sorry . . . aah, Mr. Martin, but we can't sell you any firewood. There is a ban on campfires."

She cringed as Fred grabbed her arm in a tight squeeze. "What do you mean, no campfire?" he snarled. Fear would have controlled her had the pain not been so great. "Ow! You're hurting me. Please let go," she pleaded. She saw his eyes narrow. He relaxed his grip but did not let go. He repeated his question.

She wished for someone to intercede, and Ernie's face flashed into her mind. She heard him again ask why. She attempted to regain a bit of composure. "If you will let go of my arm, I shall explain, Mr. Martin." Fred released his physical grip but she remained frozen in place. She explained about the ban being imposed and the woods being tinder-dry, and passed the blame to the DNR. Fred's face revealed nothing. He didn't smile, nod, or acknowledge that he understood. He turned quickly and retraced his steps, leaving a shaken Jessica to her own thoughts. She debated whether to call the police, and once again Ernie's face materialized before her.

Evening was quickly turning to night as Fred walked directly away from the campground and down Route 123. He didn't glance back. There was nothing there for him. Anger didn't do justice to his feelings. It wasn't madness—well, maybe madness wrapped in unspeakable wrath. It was the world against him, one versus six billion. And they would pay, oh yes, they would pay—the sick, controlling, kick-you-when-you're-down society. They would burn.

CHAPTER 9

Fred walked with putrid loathing, his fire utopia smothered in an endless dark wrath. He felt lost in a bottomless well, and everyone was stepping on his fingers as he attempted to crawl out, keeping him imprisoned and away from the things he desired. He ended up on Old Crow Hill Road and spotted a jalopy parked off the road.

A switch had flipped somewhere in Fred's noggin, and the bad man had become a monster. He'd had a complete break from humanity, and what slight compassion he previously had for his fellow citizens was lost. Wrath and fire united to become his sole purpose. Cars needed operators, operators were people, and Fred desired to make people pay for their indiscretions toward him and his pursuit of happiness.

An approaching crackle in the woods caused him to hide behind the rear of the vehicle. Crouching low, his memory flashed back to a movie he had seen years ago in which a prisoner of war was waiting in cover to blow a train bridge of dreaded Japanese. He faintly recalled a catchy tune and had to refrain from whistling out loud. Not a sound did he make, his breathing slow and silent despite the goose-pimpling he felt beneath his shirt. He waited patiently.

It was primitive, like an African rock python ambushing a warthog. Sam Wright was alive and well then gone in a blink of an eye, Fred's massive arms coiled about his neck. Dropping him into the front seat of the vehicle, Fred started whistling the tune, lost in fantasy.

Jessica would explain the brief encounter with Fred the next day to Officer English, but it wouldn't amount to much, as the police department had bigger fish to fry.

Officer English had brought Moose in as requested, but the interrogation hadn't produced much of anything that wasn't, in his humble opinion, simply speculation.

His partner, Jake, had already checked out of any solid police work, relying on his subjective leanings that pointed to Moose as the villain, and he was not relenting, spot-on sure he had the right man in his cell.

The pressure was coming down the pipe from the upper echelon, for, as you know, the motto of the RCMP is, "We always get our man."

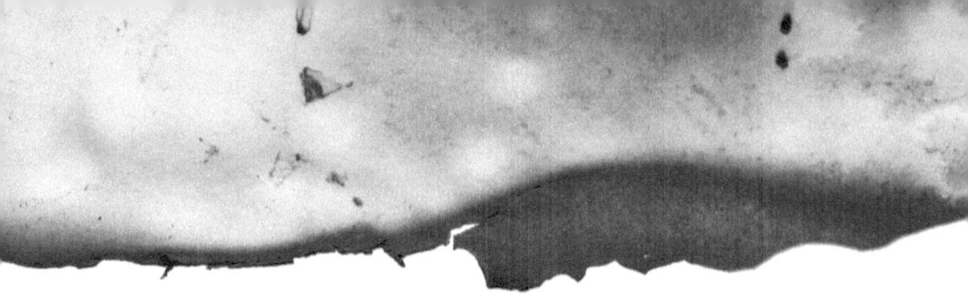

CHAPTER 10

Jake Furrow was an ambitious officer. The brutal murder was his ticket to the big time: advancement and a chance to get out of Shantyville. A green legal-size folder held the collected evidence—primary scene analysis, statements, coroner's report, pictures—all useful tools to an active investigation. However, Jake had already crossed his t's and dotted his i's. The body of Sam Wright was found within close distance to Moose's residence, who had enough hatred and motive, and his statement of, "Old geezer. He'll get his due," rang correctly. Bingo! Instant winner, pass Go, collect two hundred dollars. An arrest warrant stamped with Moose's name and recently signed by a magistrate had been issued.

His comrade in arms, Shawn English, was about two grand into a local hood. If ever there was a case for prohibition on VLTs, one had only to point to Constable English. He rarely played the lottery but was consumed by the flashing terminals and his inability to beat the machines. Sixty dollars in loonies a night didn't leave much at the end of the month. Borrowing was easier than quitting, and he knew a change of luck was just around the corner.

On his way to Moose's home, warrant of arrest in pocket, he was going through the motions, thinking of swirling cherries and blackjack. As he pulled into the driveway, he spotted Moose repairing the front steps to his weather-beaten home. Seeing who his visitor was, he quickly got up and approached the constable.

"By God, I hope you are here to tell me that you arrested that old geezer for what he done to me," Moose said. He saw indifference in English's face.

"Silky Grant, you are under arrest for the murder of Sam Wright. Anything you say can and will be used against you in a court of law."

What was this? Murder, Sam Wright . . . panic filled him. The instinct to run surfaced but his feet were rooted. From a cloud of bewildered fog, he let English cuff him. As he was loaded into the police car, some composure returned. "I hated him, but I'd never kill anyone," Moose muttered. He realized "hated" might have been a poor word selection, and said, "I'm entitled to a lawyer and a phone call," to which Constable English simply nodded.

That evening, another restless soul tossed and turned, unable to sleep. Finally admitting defeat, Ernie slouched his way into the kitchen, stumbling over the black wonder in the dark. He swung a half-hearted boot at the dog, wondering why in heaven's name anyone would own a black dog . . . or a black car, for that matter. Wasn't it dangerous enough that folks zoomed down the highway in the pitch of night with nothing more than two dim headlights showing the way? But no, let's make the bloody thing black. Might as well spray it with invisible paint. Ernie didn't drink, but was thinking he should maybe reconsider that decision.

Instead, he got a coffee going and slid a couple slices of bread into the toaster. He moved the indicator up a little from its usual "light" setting. He had read somewhere that a darker toast was good for a troubled stomach, and he had heartburn. Ernie could feel the tension building through to his bones: a lunatic on the loose, the highest fire danger index in modern history, and an infatuation that was leaving him highly confused. He smelled burning and realized he'd turned the toaster up way too high. He popped the toast—it looked like charcoal. He sighed and threw it in the trash.

By early morning he had managed only a few hours of sleep, but work didn't take any notice. He dragged himself mentally and physically up the stairs and into his office. Rangers Billings and Faulkner were both in their offices, and Ernie inquired about Don. "Where is the old man?" Billings replied Don had left earlier on his way to Freddytown, where the Department of Natural Resources headquarters was.

A quick check of the forecast showed no relief in sight for this sun-baked corner of the world. Ernie could feel the pressure of increasing anxiety on every inch of his body and swore under his breath. Maybe a little later he would take a drive out to the campground. "Just as a professional courtesy," he muttered to himself, knowing that was not completely true.

The fire situation was a ticking timebomb, and around two p.m. the alarm went off. It was a frantic call from a passerby who spotted the smoke just north of Route 123 in the vicinity of Shantyville Campground. With Don unavailable, Ernie assumed the incident-commander position and directed staff and all two- thousand-gallon tankers toward the location.

Peering north out his office window, he was astonished that he could already see huge blooms of smoke rising in the distance. Big smoke means big fire, so, knowing how tinder-dry the forests were, he radioed for air attack and the accompanying bird dog aircraft. He gave them the general co-ordinates and told them they would have no problem finding the fire with the amount of smoke in the air. Throwing a pump box on his half ton, he left Code City. Swinging west on the #123, he toggled the switch to activate his emergency lights and siren.

Fighting fire is dangerous work. This was a "type 5" fire, due to the crowning—when a fire is moving though the treetops instead of the typical on-the-ground movement, it makes containing the fire almost impossible. Ernie arrived several minutes before the tanker and took an initial look at what they were facing. He knew the area well, and immediately understood the real danger was for several camps that lay to the west of the head of this inferno. Bird Dog arrived and Ernie was on the radio. "Bird Dog, IC Doyle. Do you copy?"

"Go for Bird Dog," the pilot replied.

"Can we have the first drops on the west side of the head? I'll establish a staging area where our trucks are parked. I'll set up a hose line on our western flank."

"Ten-four, copy that," came the reply. Ernie and the crew on the ground made some progress on the flank, and the bombers managed after several hours to reduce the open flame at the head. It was getting toward dusk when the crew, with help from the Shantyville Fire Department, was able to contain the blaze. Ernie drew breaths of relief. The fire crew took another few days mopping up and looking for smokes.

On day three, Ernie declared the fire out. It had had the makings of becoming a replication of the Midland fire in the 1940s. That burn had left not only thousands of hectares scorched black, but also death for those caught unaware of the sweeping horror. It was Ernie's swift assessment of where to apply resources and the quick involvement of air attack that saved the day.

The staff at the DNR station received congratulations and letters of commendation from the province for their work. The local paper in Woodside, the Chronicle, embellished the story as RANGER HEROICS SAVE THE DAY, but staff knew it was what they had been trained for, and indeed what they were paid for. It was a calling just like any other profession, and what they were born to be.

But even the paper's portrayal of the events was minor compared to the praise and adoration being voiced by Jessica Forbes at the Shantyville Campground, and make no mistake about it, it was directed unreservedly on Ernie Doyle. As a member of the council for the local service district, she was instrumental in the celebrations planned for the newly minted victors. Gold keys to the village! On a personal note, she believed fully that Ernie had saved her campground, and she was planning a special affair to show her appreciation and approval for her rescuer. She couldn't quite put a name to her feelings, but "guardian" was emerging as appropriate.

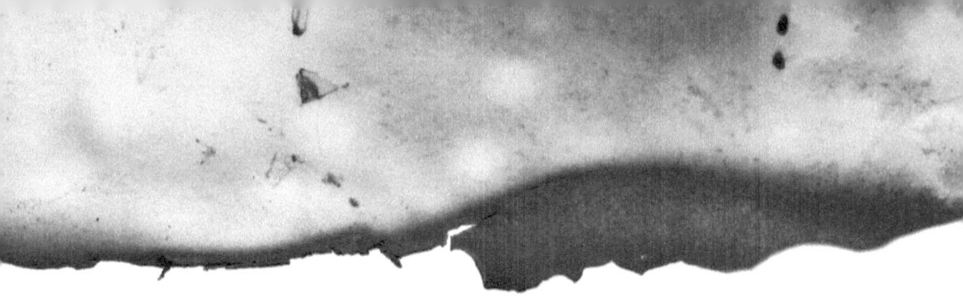

CHAPTER 11

Lieutenant Furrow took his best shots at convincing the Crown Prosecutor to lay a murder charge against Silky Grant. It didn't amount to much of a contest. Simply stated by the Crown, the case hinged on circumstantial evidence at best, and the prosecutor offered words of wisdom to not bring such a flimsy case before them again. That evening, Silky became a free man. As he exited the police station, he directed his middle finger toward Constable Furrow. A tirade of vulgar names followed, heaped on the officers with the closing argument that every charged person spouts, "I told you. You got the wrong guy!"

Beaver McPhee never missed a celebration, and the key ceremony was the first of its kind for the village. There would be lots of recyclables, and with folks in a good mood they would overeat and overdrink. The excessive boozing in Shantyville would happen anyway, as the village spigot always seemed to be turned three quarters open.

As the village gathered, Beaver nestled into a seat near the garbage containers at the rear of the village park, where he had a commanding view of the ceremony. Another unique aspect of Beaver beyond his weather-predictor capacity was, in his own words, "being able to read the heat signature of people." For instance, he noted how much longer and intense the exchange was between Forest Ranger Doyle and that lady from the campground when she presented him with his gold key. He rated the hug a 98/100 on his heat-o-metre. Beaver would keep a close eye on the pair of them, yesiree. Another point of interest was the fact that none of Ranger Doyle's family attended the event. Beaver had gleaned from an overheard conversation that his family had gone to Kim's mother's home for a visit. He was always eager for new gossip, and it was amazing how people generally overlooked his presence and would ramble on about the most private affairs as if he were not there. Standing, he headed for the steel trash barrels. Time to get to work.

Not since ten years ago had the village been so full of enthusiasm. Folks still reminisced over that event and how it began. Josiah Edwards was on his way into Shantyville from Bordertown when he spotted something on the road ahead. He slowed down a bit, expecting a moose or deer, but as he drew closer he saw it was walking on two feet. He wiped his eyes and stared at what he was certain was a Sasquatch crossing the road in front of him before disappearing into the woods on the other side. Over the next few days, more than one bewildered call was made to the DNR station reporting similar sightings. DNR was familiar with unusual sightings being reported, but most of the time the informants were under the influence. UFO to cougar sightings were reported every year with gusto by the same clientele. However, in these recent sightings, reliable and knowledgeable hunters detailed the observations.

The story made the local papers, and for a month in the summer Shantyville became the tourist destination of choice, with people flocking in to catch a glimpse of the hairy ape. The village council made the most of it with advertising, posters, and a prize offered if anyone could snap a picture of the creature.

The event fizzled when Ernie discovered in his investigation that a local idiot from the area had purchased an ape costume and started making cameo appearances. Ernie had berated him and confiscated the costume. The fool had been lucky that one of the many hunters in these parts hadn't put a bullet hole in him during one of these encounters. The village council members scratched Ernie off their Christmas mailing lists and took down all their posters.

Flammable Fred had gone into insolation after the deadly attack on Sam Wright. He needed a haven to conjure up his next assault on mankind, a secure place to work out the details. His choice was an abandoned building that had housed the former canoe factory.

It had closed back in the seventies when kayaks became the recreational vessel of choice. Invented by the Inuit of the north and initially made of seal skin, the kayak progressed to fiberglass, making them much lighter and easier to handle than the standard canoe. The building was run down and located on Granite Hill, wedged between Jillpoke Road and Route 240, heading south to the town of McAllister some twenty-six miles away. More importantly, the haven was only a mile or so as the crow flies from the centre of Shantyville.

Fred was pretty sure he would go unnoticed, just like the building that had received its last attention back in 1984, when the graduating class had spraypainted their year in big bold black numbers on the front. He had passed the high school as he left the village but he wasn't worried, as it was summer. He had detested school, with all its rules and expectations. Flashes of demanding teachers were his last thoughts as he drifted into sleep on a long wooden work bench covered in a dried epoxy resin.

Back in Ernie's world, his attention to Jessica was becoming an obsession. He tried valiantly to fight the temptation to always turn left and head westward toward the campground when leaving Code City. Over the next several days, not only did the weather continue to heat up but his desire to impress and draw attention from her consumed him. He would find himself pulling into the campground on a daily basis. He would seek her out and they would chat as they walked along the lake. Ernie loved every second of their time together. He had come up with a handle for her: his little walkie-talkie.

The trouble with budding relationships is that they work only when both parties are willing. Somewhere between the key ceremony and Ernie's constant devotion, Jessica had, for reasons only she knew, decided in her heart to cool it down between them. She had been enchanted by the dashing man in uniform and was extremely grateful that Ernie had saved her business. That she owed him beyond measure was a given, but Ernie was moving way too fast, and he *was* married, after all. She knew Kim was a lovely person, very active in her community, and their kids were adorable. The oldest was sports-driven and smart, succeeding at whatever he put his hand to, according to the teachers at the school. The middle child was taller and more reserved. Leadership qualities were distinct in him, even at his young age. Her favourite was the youngest, who seemed gentle-spirited and quiet, and so precious you wanted to take him home. Did she want to come into the middle of all that goodness? The honest answer was no.

The point was driven home when, one bright morning, she and Ernie were walking along the shore of Shingle Lake. Ernie had brought his radio and was dressed for work, just about to begin his day. "What a wonderful day, and such good company," she teased.

"Funny," he replied, "I thought it was a good day and wonderful company."

She turned to him in that moment and looked deep into his eyes. "About that," she started. "I think, maybe . . ." but before she could finish, he took her gently by the arm and, drawing her close, attempted to kiss her. "Ernie!" she exclaimed, and drew back from the embrace. He appeared shaken and embarrassed by what had transpired. She tried to get her voice back to explain but failed, and silence loomed.

"Well, I had better get going. Don't want to be late, and the fire hazard is still over the roof," he volunteered in a trembling voice.

As he turned to leave, she almost called him back but fought off the urge. Doing the moral thing, the right thing, is not always easy, she reminded herself as the green DNR truck pulled out of the driveway.

Ernie gunned the truck and headed back toward Code City. As the vehicle went from zero to sixty in six seconds, Ernie felt himself go from hero to zero. He grimaced as if poked with a hot iron. How could this have happened?

Everything between them had been going so smoothly. Ever since the fire, Jessica had showered him with flattering words and attention. It almost seemed that since the event was no longer current she had lost interest in him. In any case, Ernie was crushed, and laboured over how he could recapture that reverence and longing she had felt for him. That is the curse of grief: you either climb out of the pit or it pulls you down to the bottomless depths of despair, a place where no one in their right mind wishes to land.

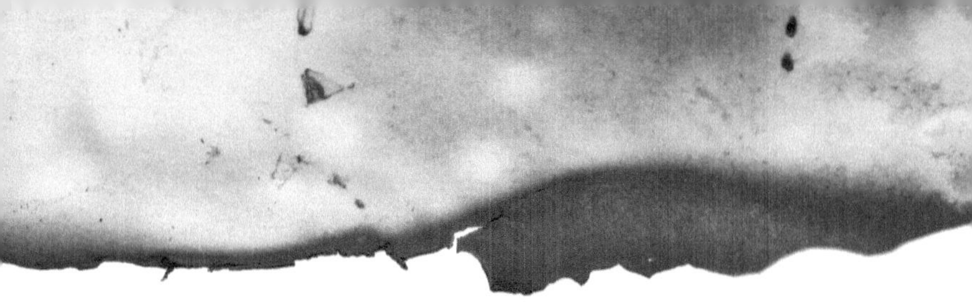

CHAPTER 12

Fred was awakened by the sound of movement outside the abandoned factory. He crept to the window overlooking the front of the building and wiped the dirt and grime from the bottom corner. It took a few seconds for his eyes to adjust to the bright sunshine and he wondered just how long he had been asleep. Slowly a car and two human forms took shape, a man and a woman. His visitors approached the end of building, where the service mast ran down the side to the power meter. There was no power at the site, as it had been disconnected back when the canoe factory had closed.

Fred could not understand why they would be there. More importantly, had someone seen him earlier? Were they looking for shelter like he had been? He spied a lengthy piece of metal pipe and grabbed it, considering multiple scenarios. The man was holding a device in front of him. The woman spoke first. "I found it," she bragged. Fred watched as they took a small grey metal box from the underside of the meter. "That's number nine for today," the man retorted, "but it looks like my GPS needs charging."

Fred had heard about geocaching from a co-worker at his previous job up north. He watched the car head back toward the village and slowly released his iron grip on his weapon. Geocaching was like an old game of hide and seek, which made him think of school days once again.

In his early years of school, grade six of the eight he would complete, he had hidden in a garbage can during a game of hide and seek. Some older kids had come along, fastened the lid, and proceeded to roll him down one of the many inclines on the school property. Upon exiting the barrel, he heard laughter from the top of the hill. The leader of this older group stopped laughing when Fred, using the lid like Captain America's shield, tagged him with a perfect throw, rendering the bully unconscious. The memory brought back one of only a few happy moments he had experienced while still in school.

His smile dissolved quickly, like cotton candy in his mouth. More serious plans were in process and Fred needed to stop at Durling's Service Station, where he had noted on his original trek through the village that they sold fireworks. A familiar notion sprang from within and announced itself once more: *Burn, baby, burn.*

Imagine Ernie, Fred, Beaver, and Jessica all coming from their separate directions and meeting at a four-way stop. Have you ever noticed that chaos usually abounds at such a stop, with nobody sure who has the right of way, or why? Call it destiny or fate, an encounter of the four was about to occur, and chaos would be claiming the right of way.

Ernie climbed out of bed. It had been a fitful sleep, populated with visions of Jessica holding him tight and breathing words of appreciation and gratitude into his ear. He glanced over at Kim and gave a huge sigh. If she could read his mind she would have jolted out of bed, thinking her husband of twenty years had gone loco, and she would have been right. What he was contemplating would have shocked him a few weeks ago. For one as dedicated to his profession as Ernie, his answer to his dilemma was profound. Ever since Adam and Eve ate of the apple in the Garden of Eden, man has battled the desires of the flesh. For mankind's first couple, that desire was securing wisdom like God. For Ernie, it was a woman named Jessica.

After visiting the washroom, Ernie went into the kitchen and started his coffee. He had to be mindful of what was to come, but he was up to the task. He had organized what he would require and picked a logical location. It was not too far from the campground, but in an area where there were no residences or current work permits to harvest trees, so no one would be in jeopardy.

Ernie's thoughts were so locked in a vacuum he didn't notice that he had burnt his toast to black. Even his taste buds failed to register this as he downed the toast and coffee. Lately, after Kim and the kids had returned from her mother's, he could feel the distance between them widening and a shift in what mattered most to him.

Fred's route began a bit differently. He had walked into the village and entered Durling's garage, which also served as a convenience store. It was his lucky day: there were two assortments of fireworks left on the shelf, the Kids Fun Pack and Bad Boy Bundle. It was an obvious choice.

The cashier was thinking of asking for ID from Fred but opted not to. Her day was going pretty good so far, and this guy made her uneasy. After ringing in the sale, she simply said, "Have a good day!" Fred was sure he would and exited the store past a sign in the window that read FIREWORKS FOR SALE, ID REQUIRED.

The Department of Natural Resources had re-issued a news bulletin closing the forests to all woods operations and banning all recreational activities due to the bone-dry conditions. Beaver McPhee's route to the four-way stop came about as a result of the ban. He had sneaked away to go fishing, disregarding the bulletin banning recreational pursuits. He was leisurely angling along Dead Brook just south of the campground, practically invisible from any passersby due to the heavy thicket of poplar that ran along the brook. Beaver had biked out to this spot because of the limited visitors that would be around. Hiding his three-speed mountain bike off a gravel road, he was having good luck catching some speckled brook trout. The maximum daily limit for trout was six, and he had just filled his quota. Beaver might have ignored the ban on recreational fishing, but he owned a moral sense of conservation and would never, ever over-fish.

He was just about back to his bike when he heard a vehicle coming down the road. He remained hidden in the brush but could see to some extent from his position. He watched surprised as a ranger truck came slowly down the road. It passed, and he viewed Ernie Doyle as the lone occupant. Beaver was glad he had taken the time to hide his transportation, for he was certain if Doyle caught him fishing he would be fined. However, the truck passed and continued on for about a hundred metres. Beaver ventured out closer to the road and watched the truck come to a full stop.

Ranger Doyle slid out of the driver's seat and looked intently up and down the road. He appeared nervous, continually looking over his shoulder, scanning the road in both directions. From the back of the pickup, he drew out his backpack and, with another heavy glance up and down the road, disappeared into the brush.

Beaver panicked. He thought maybe Ernie had seen him after all, but he could hear him occasionally breaking sticks as he advanced deeper into the thicket on the opposite side of the road. Beaver waited about ten minutes without a sound, then, though he yearned to move, he began to count off another ten. Those extra minutes brought him his reward. He was sure he smelled smoke, and out of the brush came Ranger Doyle, moving fast. He opened the door of his vehicle, threw in his backpack, and jumped in. The truck bolted, gravel flying everywhere, picking up speed quickly.

Beaver fearfully stepped onto the road. He could not only smell smoke, but he saw a white plume start to climb above the tree line. It was unimaginable to him, but his eyes were trustworthy: Ranger Doyle had started this fire. He spit chewing tobacco from between his black teeth and jumped onto his bike, heading in the opposite direction the truck had taken as fast as his little legs could pump.

About two miles down the road he let up a bit to ease a stitch in his side from his exertion. Glancing back, he could see the ever-growing black smudge against the blue sky. He renewed his pace.

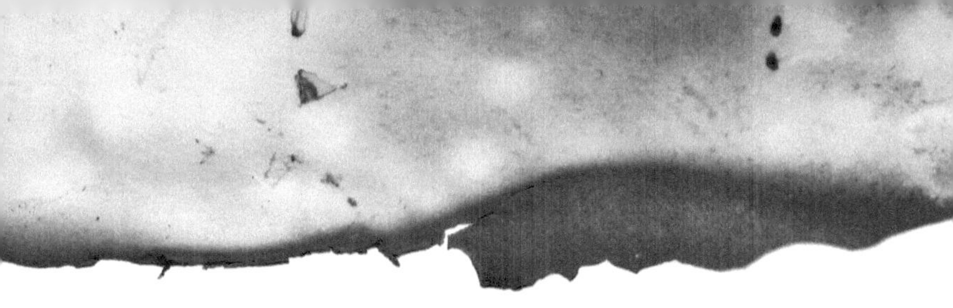

CHAPTER 13

Ranger Billings took a report from Jessica Forbes of a large smoke south of the campground. One of her yard workers noticed it while watering some of the maple saplings that had been planted earlier in the spring around the picnic area. Billings informed the boss, who told him to call it into the fire centre to see if they could get the daily spotter plane to alter its flight plan. He followed the command with his usual line: "Let Ernie know."

"Ten-four," Ernie responded on his radio. "I'll head in that direction."

Billings replied with, "What's your ETA to the fire?"

Ernie hesitated only a second, then lied. "Probably twenty minutes or so. Better get air attack en route."

Lying at this point was simple. His conscience was already subverted by what he had done. He let out a little gasp.

Flammable Fred had attempted to hitchhike to Shingle Lake. He was working himself up into a lather as vehicles failed to stop, or simply laid on their horns to his upraised thumb. By the time he reached his location just south of the lake, his feet had begun to hurt and he was drenched in sweat. He arrived at his planned location just off an old gravel lane and down a twitch road used by skidders years back, which would create small trails hauling several tree-length logs—twitches—to a main loading yard. Fred unloaded his knapsack from his aching shoulders and set about arranging the Bad Boy fireworks around him. He was giddy. He could foresee the horror this fire would bring, and life flickered back to his deadpan eyes. He imagined he smelled smoke, so intense was his dream state.

Hard to figure that a quaint place like Shingle Lake would become the base camp for a major campaign fire necessitating resources and manpower from all around the province. There had not been one in this neck of the woods for a half century. Ernie had arrived on the fire scene first and picked the location. Having her watch him work with undivided attention was like homemade bread with maple syrup: sweet and refreshing.

The equipment and tankers arrived on the scene, and Ernie, assuming the Incident Commander position, had them construct a fire line along the old Gould Lumber Company road. It was an unusual approach to not attack the head of the fire, especially with buildings in its path.

The decision struck Rangers Billings and Faulkner as strange. However, Ernie had already scouted the area and knew there was a natural marsh and springs between the fire and where they were set up. With the wind being light, there was no possible way for the fire to jump the barrier.

For Ernie, everything was going accordingly, with a good fire line formed using the old gravel road and most of his manpower and equipment. This allowed the fire fighters to direct the fire southward, away from Shingle Lake and the campground. Jessica brought Ernie a fresh drink of cool lemonade. "How is the fire situation, Ernie? Are we in danger?"

"No, I've got a handle on it," he answered. Satisfying her that the fire posed no danger with him in control was enjoyable. "You see," he explained, "fire is pinched off at the head due to the wet marsh, and we have a good fire line on one flank." He saw her eyes widen, trying to understand. He continued, "This allows us to work on the other flank, and though the fire is still hot and burning fast, it has only one direction to travel, southward and away from us."

"So we're safe. My campground is safe," she said, relieved.

"I give you my word. You can trust me, I'm here for you," he said with conviction. Her face brightened and his heart boomed with delight.

CHAPTER 14

Life is ever a mystery, like trying to do a puzzle without the picture. All we get to see are the pieces we are given, and the trick of the journey is to put the pieces into place within our lives. Sometimes we can see clearly where things fit, but more often than not we're unsuccessful.

So intent was Fred on his pursuit of madness that it did not register he was smelling smoke. He was unaware that death was rapidly advancing through the woods toward him, as his mind was overwhelmed with his private storyline of the impending doom he was planning to bring to the world. One might well imagine how wildlife feels as flames overtake them when fire breaks out on the home range.

Fred had no time to run. When he first understood the danger, when reality kicked him in the butt, the wall of fire was instantly there. There would be no rescue, no Beam me up, Scotty. A scream ripped from his lips as his clothes caught fire, echoes of his own words arriving unbidden in his mind: *Burn, baby, burn.*

Ernie had all the pieces to his puzzle in line, and he figured he knew where each should go. That all changed when the fireworks went off. From calculated observation came utter shock and disbelief in a moment. The Bad Boys lived up to their name. In every direction they shot off through the air in a spectacular show. Upon landing hundreds of yards from their spot of origin, they burst into flames in the dry forest bed. The wet-spot fire buffer of Ernie's plan didn't exist when fire travelled via air. The head of the blaze jumped and there was little those on the fire line could do. Air attack on the site had been concentrating on the western flank and had to leave the area briefly due to safety concerns with the miniature rockets doming the sky.

The fire line crew, due to a solid fire plan with an active escape route, fled to their established safety zone, which in this case was Shingle Lake Campground. The equipment and crews fell back to regroup.

All of Ernie's planning was in jeopardy. His safety zone was also functioning as the base camp, and it hinged on the concept that the fire could never reach it. In chess there is a pattern called the "fool's mate," the fastest checkmate in the game, and it relies on your opponent making a significant mistake at the start of the game. Ernie had made a similar error and had to retreat from the fire, which was now only minutes from the campground. The siren was sounded, and everyone who was not able to drive away was rounded up into other vehicles. The convoy left the area quickly, their tails between their legs.

It was checkmate at this point, and Ernie, instead of being the knight in shining armour defending his queen's property, evolved into a pawn escorting his queen out of danger's way. Instead of victory, it was utter defeat. It was touch and go to evacuate in time, and they were fortunate no lives were lost. The splendour of Shingle Lake Campground was rendered ash and charred wood.

It took endless hours of hard work by fire crews, air attack, and heavy equipment over ten days to bring the debacle under control. Another ten days was spent mopping up the smoke and cleaning hoses and equipment. Ernie was stripped of his IC position, and central command was analyzing his poor performance. There was no celebration this time in Shantyville. But good or bad news sells, and the Chronicle told the bad with unreserved delight. The paper sold out in hours and issued its first ever rerun.

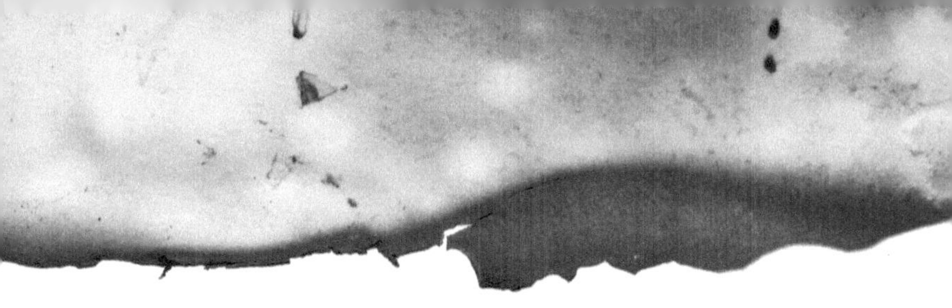

CHAPTER 15

When the smoke finally cleared, a couple of things became evident. Ernie was disciplined for gross misconduct while performing his duties; at least, that's what the letter in his personnel file read. On a deeper level, he had lost the respect of his fellow rangers, and good ol' Don relegated him to office duties. Ernie longed for the hurt to stop there. Jessica Forbes made it abundantly clear she blamed Ernie for losing her business and home in a scathing letter to the editor.

The body of one Frederick Martin was found on day five of the cleanup, along with remnants of his fireworks. The most striking issue, however, was the guilt being laid at Fred's feet, not only for the fireworks incident, but as the agent who started the disaster in the first place. It was assumed Flammable Fred simply erred, and his initial blaze rapidly overtook him while preparing his Bad Boy Bonanza.

The *Chronicle*, like most newspapers, linked the Sutton native with his questionable past as the originator of the conflagration, now nicknamed the "Fourth of July Fire."

Dumbfounded as he was at the turn of events, Ernie had a sincere belief that nobody had any idea of his real involvement, or the ghastly deed he had perpetrated. Although the outcome was distressing for him, he remedied it with the cold, hard fact that it could have been worse. The loss of the shady character that was Fred Martin was overshadowed by thoughts of a prison sentence for arson and the more serious charge of manslaughter that would accompany it. Though the paradise he had dreamed of was lost, he could take comfort in what he already possessed. To lose that would be an insurmountable journey he was ill prepared to live through.

Beaver did not stop at Shingle Lake Campground to warn them, but put as many miles as he could between himself and Ranger Doyle. Down toward the village he had biked, constantly looking over his shoulder. The fire equipment dispatched by the Department of Natural Resources had motored by him with emergency lights flashing.

Passing through Shantyville, he glanced neither right nor left. Rudy Walker, sitting across from Reno's on the steps of the old Marston Meat Shop, thought it a wonder that Beaver didn't stop or even slow down to see what was playing on the satellite TV.

Beaver was plum tired out by the time he reached his home. He took note of the smoke billowing back toward

Shingle Lake as he closed his door, and he locked it for the first time in years.

Over the next few weeks he tried his best to return to normal living; at least, normal living Beaver-style, but alas, that normal comfort would not return. He missed the big homecoming week in Woodside, the first time since returning from the war. Everything he enjoyed seemed as empty as the bottles he scavenged. His secret was rotting him from the inside out and he needed deliverance from the torment in his soul. So, when you need help for matters of the soul, who do you turn to?

In Shantyville, there was one on practically every corner.

CHAPTER 16

Beaver settled on the Baptist Church, although he attended the United Church more regularly because the congregation collectively saved their returnables for him. He was more agreeable with the minister of the Baptist flock, and besides, the Baptist folks lunched after meetings most of the time.

He was still a bit wary of telling anyone what he had witnessed, but where else could you unload all those secrets, clean your conscience, and get a good lunch at the same time? It was downstairs in the kitchen and dining hall of the church that Beaver took Pastor Cyril aside and confessed. He felt much better after releasing the burden on his soul. He reasoned that it was on the pastor's conscience now, whether or not it was reported to an official. Now on to the chicken rice soup and homemade rolls. He smacked his lips in anticipation.

Beaver might not have been so relieved if he had known anything about Baptist gossip. Pastors, like most of us, share almost everything with their spouses. It was especially necessary as the pastor and his wife are, in essence, a team ministry. Pastor Cyril's wife had a special friend whom she also confides in, and she has a mother who was a sister to Ernie himself.

So the gossip train ran the rails, and Ernie heard the news almost before poor Beaver had finished his second bowl of soup. So much for chicken soup being good for the soul. But Beaver slept well that evening, unaware he had picked the wrong church.

The morning after hearing from his sister, Ernie was in distress. The night had been long and restless. He poured some coffee and pondered his dilemma. He knew that the pastor would talk to someone about the incident, and there was not much he could do about that. He popped some bread in the toaster and puzzled over what his next course of action should be. Should he confess?

This was no longer a matter of a broken love angle with Jessica—she wanted no part of him now—but rather he needed to save his marriage and career, to say nothing of staying out of prison. A confession would sink him. He had to pinch this off at the head, just like fighting a forest fire. The answer came about the same time as he smelled the smoke from the toaster. He ejected a couple slices of completely burnt toast—he still hadn't reset the dial. It reminded him of his current situation. He could feel the heat and it was singeing every fibre of his life. But he had an idea . . .

Leaving the house, he travelled out to the site where he had started the fire. If Beaver had seen him, he must have been in the area. Ernie searched around, looking for anything Beaver might have left behind, and struck gold. Lying ten feet off the road was a fishing rod. It seemed like divine providence that it had survived the fire. Ernie smiled for the first time in days.

Sitting in his small office, Lieutenant Furrow was astonished at Ernie's statement. Arson was a criminal matter, and he asked Ernie why he had waited so long to report it. Flammable Fred was suspected to be the originator of the fire, and he was certainly a significant part of it, as he was confirmed to have been the purchaser of the fireworks.

The answer was simple: Ernie felt really bad for good ol' Beaver and didn't want him thrown in jail, but alas, his constitution and commitment to his duties as a forest ranger prevailed and he could no longer overlook what Beaver may have done. Ernie's statement on how he came across what he thought was Beaver's fishing rod while investigating the fire puzzled Furrow at the time, but then he recalled that Beaver had been spotted a bit later travelling on his bicycle away from the incident by Rudy Walker, whom he had run into in town. Ernie also mentioned in his statement that he had not seen Beaver around lately to verify that the rod was his, and it got him to thinking that maybe there was a reason for that. Ernie had the rod with him now and suggested that he and Lieutenant Furrow should go pay Beaver a visit.

The lieutenant agreed. A few intense hours later, Beaver was back on the street. His interrogation had not gone well for him, and when he claimed Forest Ranger Doyle had been the real perpetrator, he could see in their eyes and demeanor that none of this was cutting the mustard. He was informed that he would be supplied with defence counsel, paid for by the province. He would have preferred choosing his own attorney, but old-age pension and a disability cheque did not afford him enough funds for his own defence, no matter how many returnables he collected. He was charged, and it was just a matter of a trial date being set. Beaver wished that he had continued fishing beyond the daily limit on the day in question, thus avoiding his encounter with Ernie.

It saddened Ernie little that he had framed Beaver. It is odd how once a conscience is poisoned it becomes easily moulded, not only to repeat an offence, but to do it with less empathy to the harm it will cause. Such had become Ernie's character. It is often said that there is a fine line between an idiot and a genius, and when one sears their conscience, the dark side is but a bad decision away.

A few days later, Pastor Cyril did indeed approach the local RCMP detachment with the information Beaver had supplied him. It was received with the obligatory "thank you for coming." Hearsay is not evidence, and Lieutenant Furrow had the physical evidence he needed, locked up with seizure tag number 008 fastened on the shaft of Beaver's fishing rod. He had felt a great deal of satisfaction when he snapped the plastic tag in place. It was not a practice he had repeated often—tags 009 to 500 were still in the bottom drawer of his desk.

CHAPTER 17

Over the next few weeks, Ernie fell back into his regular routine. Although he was well aware of what was coming down the pipeline, he had managed the outcome of the situation and was feeling secure that everything would pan out.

Don finally took him off desk duties, and he responded to a call from a resident of Dew Settlement that an American bear hunter had threatened him and his wife for biking on a woods road only a few miles from their home. The American had suggested that the couple might get their asses shot off, as they were on ground leased by an outfitter from the Heartland area used strictly for their "sports."

Ernie proceeded to the location described by the resident and came upon the hunter standing in the middle of the dirt road. Nearby was a barrel containing bear bait. This was a typical activity of hunters who came to the province from big American cities like New York and Boston. They were unaccustomed to being in the wilderness, surrounded by trees and wild animals. This area he had been dropped off in was less than a mile from the main road. As Ernie pulled up in his marked truck, he noticed the hunter cradling his firearm and looking as nervous as a long-tailed cat in a room full of rocking chairs.

Exiting the truck, he approached the hunter and instructed him to lower his weapon and present his hunting licence. The sport complied with the order, and Ernie confirmed what he had suspected: the man was from Brooklyn. Ernie asked him where his guide was and received the reply that he had not seen him since being dropped off in the early morning hours. It was not unusual for outfitters to drop their sports early in the morning, with no idea where they are. The guide had probably also told him that it was leased ground just for his hunt, and that he would be all alone until he got picked up toward dusk, which was still a couple hours away.

Ernie explained the complaint he had received, and the hunter became agitated when Ernie told him in no uncertain tone that he was a visitor to this province, and threating citizens could lead to charges. Ernie cautioned him that he could also charge him with hunting with no guide, as the regulation stated one should be within a five-mile radius of his hunter. Neglectfully, the guide was not checking in with the sport by radio or phone, nor had he visited him at some point during the day to ensure his safety. Hunting accidents, though not common, were not rare by any stretch.

At the end of the conversation, Ernie waited to make sure the guide showed up. The hunter swore he was heading back to the city the next day, and he was not impressed that the story about the land being leased for use by American bear hunters was a downright lie. The guide finally arrived, and Ernie cornered him for his lack of professionalism and putting his sport at risk. Both the sport and guide were locked in a heated argument as Ernie headed his truck back toward Shantyville. He figured it would be a long trip for the pair back to Heartland.

Back at his office, Ernie finished up a stack of reports and recorded the day's events in his pocket diary. It felt great to be back into a routine, and it kept his thoughts camouflaged from all his lies and the framing of poor ol' Beaver.

In the Beaver home, things were different. He didn't leave the house much anymore, except for essentials such as food and drink. His hand shook profoundly as he read the official paper that had arrived in the morning mail.

It was a summons for the charge of arson—which he had expected—but it was another charge that got his hand shaking: manslaughter for the death of Frederick Martin. Beaver's whole body was shaking now. His world was upside down and spinning out of control. Panic choked him and he could not get air into his lungs. His attempt to breathe turned into a high-pitched wheeze. His eyes couldn't focus, and blackness closed in around him. He released his hold on the summons as he collapsed on the ground next to his mailbox.

The mail lady found him on her return trip and called the local ambulance base. The medics strapped Beaver onto a stretcher, loaded him, and headed to Woodside Hospital. From the emergency unit, they ran tests and found good ol' Beaver had angina, which contributed to his panic attack and fall.

The hospital ran a complete blood count and found it high. Further testing revealed cancer had migrated into his bone marrow. The outcome was not in his favour. Some of the advertisements about smoking should have been directed toward those who chewed tobacco too—at least that's what sense Beaver could make of it.

Never mind the upcoming court date, the final verdict given by the doctors was two months if he was lucky. Beaver declined the chemo, and any other treatment offered by the doctors. In a way he was happy that he would not spend his last days locked up behind bars. Besides, the nurse told him that just down the hall from his bedside, in the common area, they had free satellite TV. He asked her what they did with returnables.

CHAPTER 18

The summer faded into fall, the rain came, and folks in Shantyville started to prepare for the winter months. Harvesting of crops in the fields and the fall season of deer and game birds began in earnest. For rural folks, preparing for winter is not only hard work but a way of life. Canning vegetables, cutting fuelwood, and taking game are a necessary part of living in the country.

Ernie enjoyed the fall season best. The fire season was in the rear-view mirror, and the shorter daylight hours slowed down one's "get 'er done" pace. Life at home with Kim and the kids was a great comfort to him, but he was still restless. Thinking back over the past year and how he had come so close to losing everything should have made the present time with his family even more special.

One night, after he and Kim had played a board game with the kids and tucked them into bed, he picked up the Chronicle and eased himself onto the futon in the living room. He opened to the section of the paper called

"News from Around" and read about the break-ins at both Reno's and Jerry's Liquor Store. According to the article, they caught the culprits when they stopped at Durling's and pulled into one of the EV charging stations to try out their new TV. Guy Durling saw them roll down the window of their beat-up Corolla and attempt to plug a TV into the car-charging dock. When the RCMP arrived, both occupants were found fast asleep in the front seats. Apparently, they had already partaken of the spoils from the liquor store.

Ernie read on about some other news concerning the Wood Commission board and their fight with the provincial government over prices. But it was the next piece of news that brought him off the futon. It was a short story about the death of a Second World War vet who had passed away at the Woodside Hospital a couple of days ago—Beaver McPhee, who had resided in Shantyville after coming home from abroad. It listed a brother who was still living and his previously deceased mother and father. He had been cremated and there would be no visitation, just an internment at a later date. Donations in memory could be made to the cancer society.

Ernie did not sleep well that night. The article had awakened a semi-buried conscience. He dreamt that Beaver came to his room and told him to confess and repent, his bony finger pointing at him as he spat tobacco juice onto the bed. Pastor Cyril was vaguely outlined in the background, nodding his head in agreement. Ernie must have given out a gasp or some strange noise, for Kim shook him awake and found him drenched in sweat. "Bad Dream," was all he could mutter to her. She turned over and returned to sleep while he headed to the kitchen for a drink.

It had seemed so real and utterly terrifying that when he booted a plastic pop bottle and sent it rolling across the floor he almost screamed. It must have been one of the kids' empties that had fallen off the kitchen countertop. A death, accident, abuse, or evil secrets can only be ignored for so long. These acts need to be dealt with, or eventually the truth of it oozes out and produces major upheaval to the mind.

Ernie made a cup of coffee and popped a couple of slices of bread into the toaster. "What was that?" He glanced around and saw Beaver picking up the empty returnable from the floor, his words ringing in Ernie's ears: "Thanks for my rod back." Ernie turned away and stared straight ahead, glassy-eyed. He re-slotted his already browned toast, and within two minutes smoke and flame erupted from the toaster. His stare was rigid, unblinking, and a strangled cry escaped his lips. He was pulling his hair when Kim came into the kitchen, awakened by the smoke detector going off.

The good doctors at Woodside Memorial Hospital had their second Shantyville patient in a month. "Psychotic break" was the term they used in describing the diagnosis to Kim, a loss of contact with reality, and, in Ernie's case, delusions in which he believed with great conviction that he been visited by the dead, and he kept muttering about fires and a woman named Jessica. The most unusual detail of his break with reality was his repetition of a particular animal: a beaver . . .

One young doctor, fresh from medical school, hinted that perhaps Ernie was suffering from persecutory delusions, a condition whereby the patient believes they are being persecuted, wrongfully or rightfully. This usually happens when one believes a persecutor is out to get them.

Kim eventually took a broken Ernie home. Unable to feed or dress himself, he could not return to work and was put on sick leave indefinitely. His days were composed of Kim and an extra-mural care worker, supplied by the province, getting Ernie out of bed and dressed before spoon-feeding him his breakfast. Ernie's face was blank. It was not unlike being in a coma, but with eyes wide open.

The prescribed drugs seemed of little help, and Ernie's bewilderment grew stronger. He would lash out, flailing his arms at nothing in particular, shouting obscenities and incoherent phrases. Every now and then a word or two could be made out, but they were senselessly uttered. This was external nonsense to those around Ernie, but his internal torment was anything but. In his demented awareness, Beaver continually haunted him and threw those damnable returnables at him. His accusatory finger pointed him out, and the word guilty played over and over in Ernie's ear. The smell of burnt black toast was overwhelming.

There came a point when the family could no longer support or even bear to see poor ol' Dad like an eggplant. A close friend of Kim's had the inside pull with a nursing home down in Sutton. It would be far from home, but Kim figured maybe that was a good thing. She did not recognize her husband anymore. Arrangements were made and Ernie was transferred. The Doyle household became another statistic of the demise of the family unit within the country.

It is often said that sometimes there are worse things than dying. The words of one long-departed mother of Shantyville never rang so true: "You reap what you sow, young man."

EPILOGUE

Months have passed. Ernie Doyle remains at the nursing home in Sutton. Kim and their three boys visit regularly, although Ernie is oblivious to what is going on in their lives.

Beaver's home has been renovated and is now a picturesque country bungalow with a picket fence and young saplings bordering the well-kept lawn. It is said that a distant relative acquired the property and moved there to keep the home in the family. There is a smoke bush planted on the far edge of the home in memory of Beaver, and on rare occasions the odd discarded bottle can be found on the front lawn.

The campground is now overgrown with long grass, and there is a charred picnic table here and there echoing the aftermath of the inferno that raged through months ago. Rumour has it that another church is going to be built there.

Shantyville itself now has a scant three stores, but one of them, perhaps the busiest in the community, includes the local liquor outlet supplemented with video lottery machines. The farmers' market is still held every second Friday, and is well attended by residents, and sometimes cottage people passing through.

The DNR office is still located on the outskirts of the community, the officers putting out fires in more ways than one, as rumour and gossip are big parts of a small rural population. Oh yes, and Sasquatch has been sighted again . . .

Whatever the future holds for Shantyville, it will always be shadowed with the hauntings of Ernie Doyle, Beaver, and the notable Flammable Fred and the slogan he lived his life by: Burn, baby, burn!